For Ady, Brinley, Claire, Declan,
Ellie, Jack, Madi, and Will.

ISBN 978-0-578-81820-7 (print)
ISBN 978-0-578-81823-8 (e-book)

Library of Congress Control Number 2020924721

Illustrations: © 2021 Carissa Sorensen

Cover and interior design: Jane Dixon-Smith
jdsmith-design.com

Editor: Susan Tasaki

Elk Tooth Books
Estes Park, Colorado

Richard the Chicken Eagle

Mark Rashid

Illustrated by Carissa Sorensen

Elk Tooth Books
Estes Park, Colorado

One day, Hank the Farmer was
walking through his cornfield when
he noticed something on the ground.
An egg! But it was not like the eggs his
chickens laid. This egg was much too big!

"I wonder what kind of bird laid this egg,"
he said to himself.

Hank brought the egg home with him. He had an idea. He showed the egg to Henrietta, his best laying hen.

"Henrietta," he said. "I found this egg in the field. Would you mind sitting on it until it hatches?"

"No, no," said Henrietta. "That egg would take up too much space in my nest! I wouldn't have room for my own eggs."

Hank then went to Brinley, his second best laying hen, but she said no, too.

He took the egg to Madi, then Ady, then Ellie, then Claire, but they all turned him down because the egg was just too big!

Madi

Ady

Claire

Henrietta

Ellie

Brinley

Just as Hank the Farmer was about to give up, he heard a voice from the back of the chicken coop.

"I'll do it." It was Belinda. She was the oldest chicken in the coop and because of her age, was no longer laying many eggs. "I have room in my nest!"

"Good," Hank said. "That's settled, then."

Belinda

Belinda took her new job very seriously
and sat on the egg day and night.

One morning, as Belinda was sitting
on the egg, she felt something strange
happening. She stepped off the nest
and saw that the egg was hatching!

The other hens gathered around, clucking excitedly as the strange baby bird began to break out of the egg. First its beak came through the shell, then its head, and finally, the whole bird!

The hens didn't know what to make of the new arrival. He was big! Much bigger than the other baby chicks. And he was ugly—big eyes, a large hook on the end of his beak, and little head feathers that stuck straight up!

Hank the Farmer heard the
commotion and rushed into the chicken
coop to see what was going on.

"He hatched!" Belinda exclaimed.
"He hatched! Isn't he beautiful?"

"Beautiful is not the word I would use,"
said Henrietta. She and the other
hens waddled away.

"Well, I'll be," said Hank the Farmer.
"That's a baby eagle!"

"I don't care what he is," said Belinda.
"I'll love him and I'll raise him.
I'm going to call him Richard."

Belinda taught Richard how to hunt
for worms and scratch at the ground to
find insects to eat. Richard learned fast.
Soon, he was the best worm- and insect-
hunter in the barnyard, better even
than Roberto, the farm's rooster.

Not only did Richard learn fast, but he grew fast! In fact, he got so big that Hank the Farmer had to cut a bigger door in the henhouse so he could go in and out.

When Richard went in the henhouse to sleep, he took up so much space that there wasn't room for anybody else. The rest of the chickens didn't like that.

The chickens complained to
Roberto the Rooster, who was the
boss of the barnyard. Roberto went to
Richard and told him he could no longer
sleep in the henhouse; he would have to
sleep on top of the henhouse, by himself.
That made Richard very sad.

The next day, some of the chickens
he thought were his friends began
teasing him about his size. They called
him names and made him hunt for worms
and insects far away from the barnyard.
This also made Richard very sad.

Then one night, as Richard was sleeping on top of the henhouse, he heard a loud commotion coming from inside.

"Help, help!" he heard Henrietta yell.

"Fox!" he heard his mother, Belinda, shout.

Richard knew the chickens couldn't get out—Hank the Farmer always closed the henhouse door at night. But a fox must have somehow gotten in. He had to do something.

Lucky for the chickens, Richard was big
and strong and was able to break down
the door just in time to see the fox
holding Roberto in his mouth.

Richard became very angry.
He squinted his eyes, spread his wings,
and threw himself at the fox.

The fox dropped Roberto and ran away as fast as he could, never to return.

Suddenly, Richard was a hero, and all the chickens, even the ones who teased him, gathered around to thank him. Roberto was especially grateful.

The next day, while Richard was hunting worms and insects for his breakfast, he noticed a shadow on the ground. It was the shadow of a bird flying above him.

Richard looked up and saw
an eagle soaring high in the sky.
He was still watching the eagle
when Henrietta walked up.

"What are you looking at?" she asked.

"That bird," Richard said.
"I wish I could fly like that."

Henrietta looked up. "That's an eagle,"
she said. "The king of the sky. But you
will never fly like that because
you're just a chicken."

Richard couldn't get the eagle
out of his mind. That night, he
dreamt about flying high in the sky.

The dream was so real to Richard that
the next day, he decided to try to fly.

"You'll get hurt," some of the
chickens warned. "You can't fly,
you're only a chicken," said others.

But Richard was determined.
He climbed to the top of the barn,
the highest place he could think of, and
stood right at the edge of the roof.

"Don't do it, Richard!" the chickens
shouted from below. But for Richard,
there was no going back.

He closed his eyes tightly,
spread his wings, and jumped.

Richard dropped like a stone.
"Oh no," he thought as he fell.
"Maybe this was a bad idea!"

Just then, he heard a voice from down
in the barnyard. "Flap your wings!"
He looked down and saw Hank the Farmer
in the yard. "Flap your wings, Richard!"

"Yes," Richard thought. "Flap!"
With little time to spare, Richard began
flapping his wings as hard as he could.
Much to his delight, and just before he
hit the ground, he began to fly!

He didn't go very high at first.
But soon he was going higher
and higher and even higher!

As Richard soared through the sky, he heard a voice. "You made it! We've been waiting for you!" It was a wise old eagle, flying next to him.

"Waiting for me?" Richard said.

"Yes, we've been watching you for some time. We've been wondering when you would fly."

"I didn't know I could," Richard said. "I thought I was a chicken."

"Ah, yes," the wise old eagle replied. "But just because others tell us we are something we are not, that should never stop us from becoming who we truly are."

Hank the Farmer smiled as he
watched Richard fly away. The chickens
in the barnyard went back to digging
up worms and chasing insects.

Richard—who now knew who
he truly was—soared into the sky
alongside his new friend, the wise
old eagle, thinking about the new
adventures that lay ahead.

CPSIA information can be obtained
at www.ICGtesting.com
Printed in the USA
BVHW021428080421
604474BV00005B/71